PINGU

and the Circus

BBC CHILDREN'S BOOKS

Pingu, Pinga and Robby the seal were putting on a circus show. They had been planning it for weeks and at last the day of the show had arrived. They were busy sticking up posters to tell everyone all about it.

"Roll up, roll up! Circus, this way!" Pingu shouted.

"What fun," said two penguins. "Let's hurry along so that we can get a seat in the front row."

Robby proudly stuck up his poster. He'd been practising his circus acts for a long time now and was looking forward to the show.

Pinga was having some trouble with her poster. She just couldn't get it to stay flat on the ground. Each time she let go of it, the poster started to curl up again. In the end she had to lie on it and put a heavy stone on each corner.

It was time for the circus to begin. The audience took their seats. They were all very excited.

First of all the circus band came on. They looked a jolly troupe and played a lovely catchy tune.

Pinga blew her trumpet as hard as she could, Pingu banged loudly on his drum and Robby played the accordion with a big grin on his face.

8

Then Pingu appeared from behind the curtain with a megaphone.

"Ladies and gentlemen, welcome to the circus," he announced. "For our first act we are proud to present Robby – the incredible performing seal."

Robby emerged and began to do some amazing acrobatics. He did roly-polys and somersaults – all at high speed – and was a great hit with the audience.

Pingu announced the next act on the megaphone.
"Pinga the juggler, famous throughout the South Pole,
will now entertain you with her astonishing skills."

Pinga came forward with three brightly coloured balls. She started to juggle with them. Faster and faster and higher and higher went the balls.

Suddenly Pinga missed a ball and the whole lot came thudding to the ground.

Robby started to snigger.

"I'd like to see you juggle as well as me," said Pinga crossly and she picked up one of her balls and hurled it at Robby. It knocked his hat right off. The audience burst out laughing.

The next act began. Pinga pretended to be Robby's trainer and guided him with a stick while Robby rolled and slid along the ground. Robby barked away all the time, thoroughly enjoying himself.

15

Then he did some marvellous balancing acts with a ball on his nose.

And for his final trick, he leapt high in the air right through a hoop.

"Hup-la!" shouted Pinga.

The audience were delighted.
They clapped and clapped
while Robby and
Pinga bowed.

Now it was Pingu's turn to perform. He came on looking very big and important.

Robby played a fanfare to announce Pingu the gymnast who was going to dazzle the audience with his strength and skill.

Pingu began his act. He did all
sorts of clever things like headstands,
rolling around like a ball and forward
and back flips. The audience cheered
and clapped.

There was another fanfare as Pingu prepared himself for his final display of strength. He was going to try and lift a very heavy weight.

With a mighty heave he managed to raise the weight above his head. His body strained with the huge effort.

As soon as Pingu put the weights down again, Pinga came along and lifted them up with one arm and carried them off the stage. Pingu was furious.

"Why did you have to do that? You've made me look a complete fool," he shouted at her.

24

But the audience shrieked with laughter.

Pinga blew her trumpet to announce the next act.
She and Pingu were going to see-saw together.

Up and down they went, one after the other, until . . .

Pinga jogged the see-saw and Pingu landed –
PLOP – right in a tub of paint! The paint
splashed up and hit
Robby too.

"You look so silly," said
Pinga, laughing at them.

28

"Not half as silly as you're going to look," said
Pingu and he showered her all over with paint, too.

The audience thought it was the funniest thing they had ever seen. They hooted with laughter and stamped their feet.

"More, more!" they all shouted.

But it was time for the circus to finish. For the grand finale the circus band returned dressed as clowns.

The audience clapped along as the band played and they all agreed that it was the best circus troupe they had ever seen.

*Other PINGU books available from
BBC Children's Books:*

Pingu and the Birthday Present
Pingu Celebrates Christmas
Pingu the Chef
Pingu and the Kite
Pingu Looks After the Egg
Pingu and the Messy Meal
Pingu and the Spotty Day

Pingu the Postman Wheelie Book
Pingu Lift-the-Flap Book
Pingu Address Book
Pingu Birthday Book

Fun with Pingu Activity Book
Fun with Pingu Christmas Activity Book
Fun with Pingu Colouring Book
Fun with Pingu Press-Out and Story Book
Fun with Pingu Sticker and Story Book

Pingu Mini Books
Pingu Chunky Books